Here's what kids have to say to
Mary Pope Osborne, author of
the Magic Tree House series:

I want you to write 999 [text obscured by barcode]
—Tyler C.

I let my teacher read o [text obscured] *d
it was her most favorite book.*—Jackie F.

*I love your books so much! My favorite is all of
them!*—Lauren D.

*I love your Magic Tree House series. I feel as if
I could walk right through the books.*—Levi H.

*I wish I could collect every one of your books,
and I hope you make millions more.*—Claire M.

*Whenever I read a Magic Tree House book, it
makes my mind go off on an adventure.*—Jeff D.

*I wish I could spend my life reading the Magic
Tree House series.*—Juliette S.

*I have now read quite a few of your series. I feel
proud that I have read so many books. I am
telling all my friends.*—Meredith M.

*I really like your Magic Tree House books. They
are making me happier than a hyena.*
—Natalie D.

Parents and teachers love Magic Tree House books, too!

As a parent, I thank you for writing stories filled with adventures, fun, and valuable lessons.—M. Nagao

You have made a reader out of my 8-year-old son! I had the thrilling experience yesterday of watching him walk from the car to the front door, his nose in your book the whole way.—M. Houghton

Your Magic Tree House series may inspire me to go back and teach elementary students and gear an entire curriculum around your series!—J. Hendrickson

Thanks for writing such great books! Not only have your books motivated our class to want to read better, but our class has motivated other classes to do the same! At least six other classrooms have ordered the Magic Tree House books for next year.
—Mrs. Kennedy

My class has just discovered your wonderful Magic Tree House series! They are thrilled, scared, entertained, and mesmerized by the adventures of Jack and Annie!
—B. Paget-Puppa

I can't tell you how much my students' success at reading the Magic Tree House books has had an impact upon their learning in other classrooms. I even have parents calling me to inquire what I have done to their child, who previously didn't know how to read!—P. Lorensen

Dear Readers,

For several years I've wanted Jack and Annie to visit Native American people in the 1800s. I wasn't sure which tribe they should visit, for there are many different Native American tribes, and each is unique with its own customs, language, and way of life.

Finally, I settled on the Lakota, a tribe of the Great Plains. My research was a bit difficult, though, because I discovered that there are several groups of Lakota Indians, each different from the other. Also, many Lakota customs and beliefs have never been written down, so no one can say for sure what their way of life was actually like over a century ago.

But in <u>Buffalo Before Breakfast</u>, I have tried to share with you the most basic information I've learned about the traditional ways of the Lakota people. Jack, Annie, and I feel privileged to have spent a short "visit" with these interesting people. And we hope that you will, too.

All my best,

Mary Pope Osborne

Buffalo Before Breakfast

by Mary Pope Osborne

illustrated by Sal Murdocca

A STEPPING STONE BOOK™

Random House · New York

For Natalie,
kind and funny grandmother
of Andrew and Peter

Text copyright © 1999 by Mary Pope Osborne.
Illustrations copyright © 1999 by Sal Murdocca.

www.randomhouse.com/kids

Library of Congress Cataloging-in-Publication Data

Osborne, Mary Pope.
Buffalo before breakfast / by Mary Pope Osborne ; illustrated by Sal Murdocca.
p. cm. — (Magic tree house ; #18) "A stepping stone book." Summary: The magic
tree house takes Jack and his sister Annie to the Great Plains, where they learn
about the life of the Lakota Indians.
ISBN 978-0-679-89064-5 (pbk.) — ISBN 978-0-679-99064-2 (lib. bdg.)
[1. Time travel—Fiction. 2. Magic—Fiction. 3. Tree houses—Fiction. 4. Dakota
Indians—Fiction. 5. Indians of North America—Great Plains—Fiction.]
I. Murdocca, Sal, ill. II. Title. III. Series: Osborne, Mary Pope. Magic tree house
series ; 18.   PZ7.O81167Bu 1999 [Fic]—dc21 98-37089

Printed in the United States of America   41

Random House, Inc. New York, Toronto, London, Sydney, Auckland

A STEPPING STONE BOOK and colophon are trademarks of Random House, Inc.

Contents

Buffalo Before Breakfast

Prologue

One summer day in Frog Creek, Pennsylvania, a mysterious tree house appeared in the woods.

Eight-year-old Jack and his seven-year-old sister, Annie, climbed into the tree house. They found it was filled with books.

Jack and Annie soon discovered that the tree house was magic. It could take them to the places in the books. All they had to do was point to a picture and wish to go there.

Along the way, Jack and Annie discovered that the tree house belongs to Morgan le Fay. Morgan is a magical librarian from the time of King Arthur. She travels through time and space, gathering books.

In Magic Tree House Books #5–8, Jack and Annie helped free Morgan from a spell. In books #9–12, they solved four ancient riddles and became Master Librarians.

In Magic Tree House Books #13–16, Jack and Annie had to save four ancient stories from being lost forever.

In Magic Tree House Books #17–20, Jack and Annie must be given four special gifts to help free a mysterious dog from a magic spell. They have already received one gift on a trip to the *Titanic*. And now they are about to set out in search of the second gift. . . .

1

Teddy's Back!

Arf! Arf! Arf!

Jack finished tying his sneakers. Then he looked out his bedroom window.

A small dog stood in the early sunlight. He had floppy ears and scruffy brown fur.

"Teddy!" said Jack.

Just then, Annie ran into Jack's room.

"Teddy's back!" she said. "It's time."

It was time for their second mission to help free the little dog from a spell.

Jack threw his notebook and pencil into his backpack. Then he followed Annie downstairs and past the kitchen.

"Where are you two going?" their mom called.

"Outside," said Jack.

"Breakfast will be ready soon," she said. "And Grandmother will be here any minute."

"We'll be right back," said Jack. He loved his grandmother's visits. She was kind and funny. And she always taught them new things.

Jack and Annie slipped out the front door. Teddy was waiting for them.

Arf! Arf! he barked.

"Hey, where did you go last week?" Jack asked.

The small dog wagged his tail joyfully.

Then he ran up the sidewalk.

"Wait for us!" Annie shouted.

She and Jack followed Teddy up the street and into the Frog Creek woods.

They ran between the trees. Wind rattled the leaves. Birds swooped from branch to branch.

Teddy stopped at a rope ladder that hung from the tallest oak tree in the woods. At the top of the ladder was the magic tree house.

Jack and Annie stared up at it.

"No sign of Morgan," said Annie.

"Let's go up," said Jack.

Annie picked up Teddy. She carried him carefully up the ladder. Jack climbed after her.

Inside the tree house, Teddy sniffed a silver pocket watch on the floor. Beside it was the note that Morgan had written to Jack and Annie.

Annie picked up the note and read it aloud:

This little dog is under a spell and needs your help. To free him, you must be given four special things:

A gift from a ship lost at sea,
A gift from the prairie blue,
A gift from a forest far away,
A gift from a kangaroo.
Be brave. Be wise. Be careful.

"We've got the first special thing," said Annie, "the gift from a ship lost at sea."

"Yeah," said Jack. He picked up the silver pocket watch.

The time on the watch was 2:20—the time the *Titanic* had sunk.

Jack and Annie stared at the watch.

Arf! Arf!

Teddy's barking brought Jack back from his memories.

"Okay," Jack said. He sighed and pushed his glasses into place. "Now it's time for the gift from the prairie blue."

"What's that mean?" said Annie.

"I'm not sure," said Jack. He looked around the tree house. "But I bet that book will take us there."

He picked up a book in the corner. The cover was a picture of a wide prairie. The title was *The Great Plains*.

"Ready?" Jack said.

Teddy yipped and wagged his tail.

"Let's go," said Annie. "The sooner we free Teddy, the better."

Jack pointed at the cover.

"I wish we could go there," he said.

The wind started to blow.

The tree house started to spin.

It spun faster and faster.

Then everything was still.

Absolutely still.

2

Ocean of Grass

Early sunlight slanted into the tree house. The cool breeze smelled of wild grass.

"Oh, man," said Jack. "These are neat clothes."

Their jeans and T-shirts had magically changed. Jack had on a buckskin shirt and pants. Annie wore a fringed buckskin dress.

They both wore soft leather boots and coonskin caps. Jack's backpack was now a leather bag.

"I feel like a mountain man," he said.

"All you're missing is a mountain," said Annie. She pointed out the window.

Jack and Teddy looked out.

The tree house sat in a lone tree in a vast golden prairie. The sun was rising in the distance.

Wind whispered through the tall yellow grass. *Shh—shh—shh*, it said.

"We need a gift from the prairie blue," said Jack.

"I bet that means the sky," said Annie, looking up.

"Yep," said Jack. The sky was growing bluer as they watched. "But how are we supposed to get it?"

"Just like last time," said Annie. "We have to wait till someone gives it to us."

"I don't see any sign of people out there," said Jack.

He opened their book and read aloud.

> **The Great Plains are in the middle of the United States. Before the 20th century, this vast prairie covered nearly a fifth of America's land. Some called it "an ocean of grass."**

Jack pulled out his notebook.

"Come on," said Annie.

She picked up Teddy and carried him down the ladder.

Jack quickly wrote:

Great Plains — lots of land

"Wow, this *is* like an ocean of grass," Annie called from below.

Jack slipped the Great Plains book and his notebook into his leather bag and climbed down.

When he stepped onto the ground, the grass came all the way up to his chest. It tickled his nose.

"*Ah-ah-CHOO!*" he sneezed.

"Let's go swimming in the grass ocean," said Annie.

She started off with Teddy under her arm.

The wind blew gently as Jack hurried after her. All he could see was rolling waves of grass.

They walked and walked and walked. Finally, they stopped to rest.

"We could walk for months and never see anything but grass," said Jack.

Arf! Arf!

"Teddy says there's something great up ahead," said Annie.

"You can't tell what he's saying," said Jack. "He's just barking."

"I *can* tell," said Annie. "Trust me."

"We can't walk all day," said Jack.

"Come on," said Annie. "Just a little farther." She started walking again.

"Oh, brother," said Jack.

But he kept going through the tall, rippling grass. They went down a small slope, then up a small rise. At the top of the rise, Jack froze.

"Wow, that *is* great," he whispered.

"Told you," said Annie.

3

Black Hawk

Jack stared at a circle of tepees ahead. Busy people in buckskins moved about the circle. Horses and ponies grazed nearby.

Jack took out their research book and found a picture of the tepees.

He read:

> In the early 1800s, many different Native American tribes lived on the Great Plains. The Lakota were the

**largest tribe. They lived mostly in the
areas we now call North Dakota,
South Dakota, and Minnesota.**

Jack pulled out his notebook and wrote:

*early 1800s—Lakota were
largest tribe of Great Plains*

Behind Jack and Annie, a horse neighed.
They turned. A horse and rider were
heading toward the tepee camp.

The sun was very bright behind the rider. Jack could only see the outline of a body with a bow and a quiver of arrows on his back.

Jack quickly flipped through the book. He found a picture of a man on horseback carrying a bow and arrows. Below the picture it said LAKOTA WARRIOR.

Jack read:

> Everything changed for the Native
> Americans of the Great Plains after
> white settlers arrived in the mid-1800s.
> Fighting broke out between Lakota
> warriors and white soldiers. By the
> end of the 1800s, the Lakota were
> defeated. They lost both their land and
> their old way of life.

Jack looked back at the rider. The warrior was coming closer.

"Get down," he whispered.

"Why?" said Annie.

"This might be a time when the Indians

are fighting with the settlers," said Jack.

The grass rustled as the warrior passed by them. His horse neighed again.

Arf! Arf!

"Shh!" whispered Jack.

But it was too late. The warrior had heard Teddy's barking. He galloped toward them, grabbing his bow.

"Wait!" shouted Jack. He jumped up from the grass. "We come in peace!"

The rider halted.

Now Jack saw that he was only a boy on a pony. He couldn't have been more than ten or eleven.

"Hey, you're just a kid," Annie said, smiling.

The boy didn't smile back. But he did lower his bow while he stared at Annie.

"What's your name?" she asked.

"Black Hawk," he said.

"Cool name," said Annie. "We're Jack and Annie. We're just visiting. We live in Frog Creek, Pennsylvania."

Black Hawk nodded. Then he turned his pony around and started toward the Lakota camp.

"Hey, can we come with you?" called Annie.

Black Hawk looked back.

"Yes," he said. "Meet my people."

"You mean your parents?" asked Annie.

"No, they died long ago," said Black Hawk. "I live with my grandmother."

"Oh, I'd like to meet your grandmother," said Annie. "I'm going to see my grandmother today, too."

Black Hawk nudged his pony forward again. Annie followed with Teddy.

Jack didn't move.

What if the Lakota are at war with the white settlers? he worried. *What if they think we're enemies?*

"Annie!" Jack called softly. "We don't know if it's safe or not!"

But Annie just waved for him to come on.

Jack sighed. He opened the research book and quickly flipped through the pages. He wanted information about how to act with the Lakota.

On one page, he read:

> **Good manners to the Lakota mean speaking as few words as possible and sharing gifts when visiting.**

On another page, he read:

The Lakota admire those who do not show fear.

Jack's favorite piece of information was:

Holding up two fingers means "friend."

Jack put the book away. He ran to catch up with Annie.

Annie was telling Black Hawk all about their grandmother. The boy listened silently.

"Annie," Jack whispered. "I just read that it's good manners to be quiet. And we should give gifts and not show fear. Also, holding up two fingers means 'friend.'"

Annie nodded.

"Got that?" said Jack.

"Sure," she said. "No talking, no fear, no problem."

Jack looked up. He caught his breath.

Ahead of them, the people at the campsite had stopped what they were doing. All eyes were turned to Jack and Annie.

Jack quickly held up two fingers. Annie did the same.

4

Good Manners

Black Hawk led Jack and Annie toward the tepees. Everyone kept watching them.

Jack couldn't tell what anyone was thinking. No one looked angry. But no one looked happy, either.

Jack wondered how to appear brave.

He glanced at Annie. She walked tall and straight. Her chin was up. Her face was calm.

Jack straightened his shoulders. He lifted his chin, and he felt braver.

Black Hawk stopped and slid off his pony. The pony headed for the grazing pasture.

Then Black Hawk led them to a tepee. It was covered with buffalo designs.

"Grandmother is inside," Black Hawk said to Jack and Annie.

Inside, the tepee looked like a small round room. A fire burned in the center. Smoke rose through a hole at the top.

An old woman sat on animal skins. She was sewing beads onto a moccasin.

She looked up at Jack and Annie.

"Grandmother," said Black Hawk. "This is Jack and Annie from Frog Creek, Pennsylvania."

Jack and Annie both held up two fingers for "friend."

Grandmother raised two fingers also.

Then Jack took off his coonskin cap. He gave it to Grandmother.

She put the cap on her head, then laughed. Jack and Annie laughed, too.

Grandmother's laughter and kind face reminded Jack of his own grandmother.

"You wish to learn our ways," she said.

Jack and Annie nodded. Jack could tell she was wise.

Grandmother stood and left the tepee. They followed her.

Outside, everyone was busy again. They all seemed to know that Jack and Annie weren't enemies.

Jack looked around the camp.

Men and boys carved bows. Women and girls pounded meat and sewed clothes. One girl was adding claws to a buckskin shirt.

"The bear claws will give her the strength of the bear," said Grandmother. "She will sew on hawk feathers, elk teeth, and porcupine quills, too. All will give her the power of the animals."

Jack pulled out his notebook and wrote:

sew bear claws to shirt

"I have strong animal power when I go on a buffalo hunt," Black Hawk said proudly.

"What do you mean?" asked Jack.

"I will show you," said Black Hawk. "Wait."

Black Hawk went back inside the tepee.

Annie turned to Grandmother.

"Why does he hunt the buffalo?" she asked.

"The buffalo gives our people many gifts," said the old woman. "Food from his body. Tepees from his skin, tools from his bones."

Jack started making a list.

"Cups from his horns," Grandmother went on. "Ropes from his hair. Even winter sleds from his ribs."

Jack finished his list.

<u>buffalo</u>
skin—tepee
bones—tools
horns—cups
hair—ropes
ribs—sleds

"That reminds me of the seal hunter in the

29

Arctic," said Annie. "He used all the gifts from the seal's body. He didn't waste a thing."

Just then, Teddy began growling and barking.

Jack and Annie turned around. They both gasped.

Coming out of Grandmother's tepee was a huge wolf!

5

Sunlight and Midnight

The wolf had yellow eyes and sharp teeth.

Teddy snarled and barked. Annie rushed forward to grab the little dog.

Suddenly the wolf stood up on its hind legs!

"Yikes!" said Annie.

She leaped back.

Then she and Jack started to laugh.

The fierce wolf was Black Hawk wearing a wolf's hide! His head came out through a slit near the wolf's neck. He gave Jack and Annie a little smile.

"That's a great wolf suit," said Annie.

"Why do you wear that?" asked Jack.

"The wolf is the most powerful hunter of the buffalo," said Black Hawk. "When I wear his skin, I feel his strength."

"Wow," said Annie.

Black Hawk looked at his grandmother.

"May I show them the buffalo now?" he said.

"Only *show*," said Grandmother. "Do not hunt. We have enough meat today."

She looked back at Jack and Annie.

"Lakota never take more buffalo than we need," she said.

"That's good," said Annie.

Black Hawk handed his wolf skin to

Grandmother. Then he ran to the grazing ponies.

He climbed on his. Then he herded two ponies, one black and one yellow, over to Jack and Annie.

"Hi, Midnight. Hi, Sunlight," said Annie, naming the ponies. She patted their noses.

"Annie," whispered Jack. "How are we going to ride without saddles or reins?"

"Just hold on to their manes," she said, "and grip with your legs. Watch."

Annie threw her arms around Midnight's neck. She slung her leg over the pony's back and pulled herself up.

"I'll carry Teddy in the bag," Annie said.

Jack picked up Teddy and slipped him inside the leather bag. He handed it to Annie, who hung it over her shoulder. Teddy's head peeked out of the bag.

Arf! he barked.

"Giddy-up, Midnight!" said Annie. The pony started to walk away.

"Wait—" said Jack.

He turned to Black Hawk. He had just a few questions.

Black Hawk let out a wild whoop and took off, too.

Jack took a deep breath. He threw his arms around Sunlight's neck. Then he slung his leg over the pony's back.

The pony started to move!

"Wait—wait!" said Jack. He hopped on one foot, trying to keep up.

The pony stopped.

Slowly, Jack pulled himself onto Sunlight's back. He gripped the pony's mane. Then he carefully reached up and pushed his glasses into place.

He looked over his shoulder. Grandmother was watching.

She nodded at him.

Lakota people admire those who do not show fear, Jack remembered.

He liked Grandmother. He wanted her to admire him. He let out a wild whoop, and Sunlight took off like the wind.

The whoop made Jack feel braver.

He held tightly to Sunlight's mane. They caught up with Black Hawk and Annie, and together they all rode through the tall grass.

Shadows of clouds swept over the plains. They looked like giant dark birds spreading their wings.

Black Hawk's pony stopped at the top of a

grassy slope. Sunlight and Midnight halted right behind him.

Jack couldn't believe his eyes.

Before them were thousands and thousands of grazing buffalo.

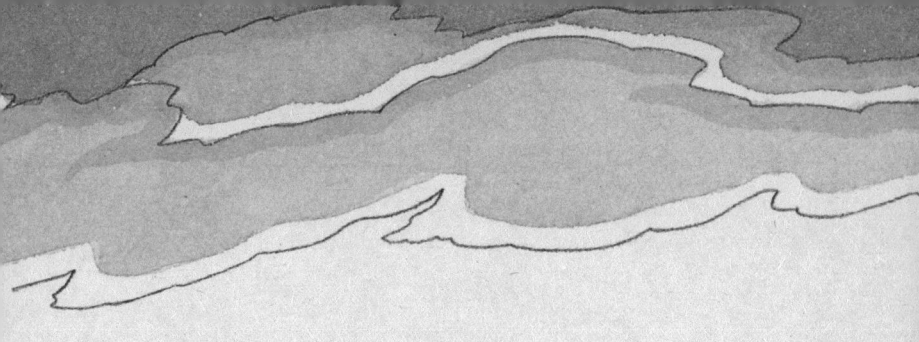

6

Stampede!

"Wow," whispered Jack and Annie together.

Black Hawk looked silently at the grazing buffalo.

"Hand me the research book," said Jack.

Annie lifted Teddy out of the bag. Then she slid the book out and gave it to Jack.

He found a picture of a buffalo herd. He read to himself.

> The true name of the buffalo is "bison." At the beginning of the 1800s, there

were 40 million bison on the Great
Plains. One hundred years later, there
were less than 300. Almost all had been
killed by white hunters and soldiers.

Jack looked back at the vast herd. As far
as he could see, there was nothing but buffalo.

Now Jack knew for certain they'd come to the time *before* the white settlers and soldiers had arrived, *before* the end of the great buffalo herds.

"I have been on many hunts," Black Hawk said, his eyes still on the buffalo.

"Were you scared?" said Jack.

Black Hawk shook his head.

"You're really brave," said Annie.

Black Hawk smiled proudly.

"I will show you how a brave hunter moves," he said.

He slid off his pony.

"Wait, your grandmother said not to hunt," said Annie. "Plus, you don't have your wolf suit."

"I am not afraid," said Black Hawk.

"I don't think you should go down there,"

said Jack. "There's no grownups around."

But Black Hawk wasn't listening.

He began creeping on all fours toward the buffalo.

"I have a feeling something bad is going to happen," said Annie.

Jack had the same feeling. He looked back at the book.

A bison can weigh two thousand pounds and stand six feet high. If one becomes alarmed by a hunter, he might start running and set off a terrifying stampede.

Jack looked back at Black Hawk. He was creeping closer and closer to the herd.

Jack's heart pounded. He wanted to shout, *Come back!* But he didn't want to scare any of the huge, fierce-looking animals.

Keeping his eyes on Black Hawk, Jack handed the plains book to Annie. She slid it back into the bag beside Teddy.

Black Hawk stopped just as he was passing the nearest buffalo. His eyes squeezed shut. His nose wrinkled up. His mouth opened.

"What's he doing?" asked Jack.

"*Ah-ah-CHOO!*" Black Hawk sneezed.

"Uh-oh," said Annie.

The huge buffalo jerked its head up. It made a low, moaning sound. Then it pointed its horns and charged!

"Watch out!" cried Jack.

Black Hawk threw himself out of the way of the charging buffalo.

A ripple went through the herd as other shaggy animals looked up.

Suddenly, Teddy jumped out of Annie's arms. He landed in the tall grass and ran toward the buffalo.

"Teddy!" shouted Annie.

The dog tore down the hill. He bounded along the edge of the herd, barking furiously.

"Teddy, come back!" cried Annie.

She slid off her pony and ran after Teddy.

Jack tried to see Black Hawk.

The boy was still dodging the running buffalo. He looked tired.

Jack took a deep breath.

"Go to Black Hawk!" he said, nudging Sunlight with his knees.

The golden pony charged down the slope. He ran between the buffalo.

"Black Hawk!" Jack shouted.

Black Hawk started running toward Sunlight. The buffalo swerved behind him.

Sunlight slowed as Black Hawk got near. The boy threw himself over the golden pony's back. He held on to Jack as Sunlight veered away from the buffalo and ran back up the slope.

"Where's Annie?" Jack cried as they reached the top.

"There!" said Black Hawk, pointing.

Annie was surrounded by buffalo—*calm* buffalo. She was patting them and talking to them. The buffalo near her had stopped running, too.

The ones beyond those started to calm down . . . then others . . . until all the buffalo had stopped running. They began grazing again as if nothing had happened.

7

White Buffalo Woman

"She has good medicine," said Black Hawk.

"Annie doesn't have any medicine," Jack said. "She just has a way with animals."

Black Hawk was silent. He climbed back on his waiting pony. Then he rode down toward Annie.

Jack followed. Annie's pony trailed behind.

Annie turned to Jack and Black Hawk as they rode up to her. On her face was a look of amazement.

"You wouldn't believe what happened!" she said.

"You stopped the stampede," said Black Hawk.

"But it wasn't just me," said Annie.

"What do you mean?" asked Jack.

"I was trying to find Teddy," said Annie, "and I got in the way of the buffalo. I couldn't escape. So I held up my hands and shouted, '*Stop!*' Then, out of nowhere, a beautiful lady in a white leather dress came to help me."

"You saw a lady in white?" asked Black Hawk. His eyes had grown wide.

"Yes!" said Annie. "She held up *her* hands, and the buffalo stopped running. Then she disappeared."

"Where's Teddy?" said Jack.

Annie gasped.

"I don't know! I forgot about him!" she said. "Teddy! Teddy!"

Arf! Arf!

The little dog came bounding out of the grass toward them.

Annie scooped him up. Teddy licked her face all over.

"Where did you go?" Annie asked him. "Did you see the beautiful lady, too?"

"That lady does not live on this earth," Black Hawk said softly.

"What do you mean?" said Annie.

"You saw the spirit of White Buffalo Woman," he said.

"What do you mean, *spirit?*" said Jack. "You mean like a ghost?"

Black Hawk turned his pony around.

"Let us go back," he said. "We must tell Grandmother."

Annie put Teddy in Jack's bag. Then she climbed on her pony, and they took off.

Behind them, the buffalo grazed peacefully on the plains.

8

Sacred Circle

The sun was going down as the three ponies galloped for home. The deep blue sky was streaked with golden red light.

Back at the Lakota camp, the circle of tepees glowed in the setting sun. People were gathered around a large fire.

Black Hawk led Jack and Annie to the camp. They got off their ponies and went over to the fire.

Grandmother rose to greet them.

"You have been gone a long time," she said.

Black Hawk looked her bravely in the eye.

"Grandmother, I tried to hunt the buffalo alone," he said. "One charged at me, but Jack saved my life. Then Annie and White Buffalo Woman stopped all the other buffalo from a stampede."

"Let this be a lesson to you," Grandmother said sternly. "Your pride led you to show off. Showing off made you behave foolishly. Your foolishness frightened a buffalo. He frightened others. One thing always leads to another. Everything is related."

"I am sorry," said Black Hawk. He hung his head. "I have learned."

Jack felt sorry for Black Hawk.

"I make mistakes sometimes, too," he said softly.

"Me too," said Annie.

Grandmother looked at Jack and Annie.

"Buffalo Girl and Rides-Like-Wind showed great courage today," she said.

Jack smiled. He loved his new Lakota name: *Rides-Like-Wind*.

"We welcome you to our family," said Grandmother.

The evening shadows spread over the camp. Someone began beating a drum. It sounded like a heartbeat.

"Come, sit with us in our circle," said Grandmother.

They sat with her near the warm fire. A cool breeze blew sparks into the gray twilight.

An old man held a long pipe up to the sky.
He pointed it to the east, the south, the west,
and the north.

Then he passed the pipe to the next man

in the circle. The man put the pipe to his lips and blew smoke into the golden firelight. Then he passed it on.

"The smoke from the sacred pipe joins all

things to the Great Spirit," Grandmother said to Jack and Annie.

"The Great Spirit?" asked Annie.

"The Great Spirit is the source of all things in the sacred circle of life," said Grandmother. "It is the source of all spirits."

"What spirits?" asked Jack.

"There are many," said Grandmother. "Wind spirits, tree spirits, bird spirits. Sometimes they can be seen. Sometimes not."

"What about the White Buffalo Woman?" said Jack. "Who is she?"

"She is a messenger of the Great Spirit," said Grandmother. "He sent her when the people were starving. She brought the sacred pipe so that our prayers could rise to the Great Spirit. He answers by sending us the buffalo."

"Why do you think White Buffalo Woman came to me?" asked Annie.

"Sometimes courage can summon help from the beyond," Grandmother said.

She pulled a brown-and-white feather from a small buckskin bag.

She put the feather on the ground in front of Jack and Annie.

"This is a gift for you," she said. "An eagle's feather for your courage."

Arf! Arf! Teddy wagged his tail.

Jack and Annie smiled at each other. The eagle's feather was their "gift from the prairie blue."

Their mission was complete.

The chanting and drumbeats grew louder and louder. Then they stopped.

The old man held the pipe up to the sky.

"All things are related," he said.

The pipe-smoking ceremony was over.

The sky was dark and filled with stars.

One by one, people rose from the circle and went to their tepees.

Jack put the eagle's feather in his bag and yawned.

"We better go home now," he said.

"You must rest first," said Grandmother. "You can leave in the dawn."

"Good plan," said Annie. She was yawning, too.

They went with Grandmother and Black Hawk to their tepee.

Grandmother pointed to two buffalo robes that lay to one side of the still-burning fire. Jack and Annie stretched out on them. Teddy snuggled between them.

Grandmother and Black Hawk lay on robes across from them.

Jack watched as the bluish white smoke rose from the fire. It went up through the tepee hole and into the endless starry sky.

Jack listened to the wind blowing through the grass: *Shh—shh—shh.*

It's the voice of the Great Plains, he thought. Then he drifted off to sleep.

9

Lakota School

Jack felt Teddy licking his cheek.

He opened his eyes. Gray light came through the smoke hole.

The fire was out. The tepee was empty.

Jack jumped up. He grabbed his bag and hurried outside with Teddy.

In the cool light before dawn, everyone was taking down their tepees. They were loading them onto wooden platforms strapped to two poles. The poles were pulled by horses.

Grandmother and Black Hawk piled tools and clothes onto their platform.

Annie stuffed buffalo meat into a rawhide bag.

"What's happening?" Jack asked.

"It is time to follow the buffalo," said Grandmother. "We will camp somewhere else for a few weeks."

Jack pulled out his notebook. He still had many questions. But he tried to choose just a few.

"Can you camp anywhere?" he asked. "Even when you don't own the land?"

Black Hawk laughed.

"People cannot own land," he said. "The land belongs to the Great Spirit."

Jack wrote in his notebook:

land owned by Great Spirit, not people

"What about school?" said Jack. "Don't you have to go to school?"

"What is school?" Black Hawk said.

"It's a place where kids go to learn things," Jack explained.

Black Hawk laughed again.

"There is not only one place to learn," he said. "In camp we learn to make clothes, tools, and tepees. On the plains we learn to ride and hunt. We look at the sky and learn courage from the eagle."

Jack wrote:

Lakota school is everywhere

Grandmother turned to Jack and Annie.

"Will you walk with us toward the sunset?" she asked.

Jack shook his head.

"We have to go the other way," he said, "toward the sunrise."

"Thank you for the eagle's feather," said Annie.

"Let your thoughts rise as high as that feather," said Grandmother. "It is good medicine."

"What does that mean?" Jack asked. *"Good medicine?"*

"Good medicine connects you to the world of the spirits," she said.

Jack nodded. But he still didn't really understand.

"Good-bye, Buffalo Girl and Rides-Like-Wind," said Grandmother. "We wish you a safe journey."

Jack and Annie waved. Then they started walking back the way they'd come.

Teddy ran ahead of them.

At the top of the rise, they looked back.

Grandmother, Black Hawk, and the rest of the tribe were watching.

Jack and Annie both held up two fingers for "friend." Then they took off down the slope.

They ran across the prairie . . . through the tall, whispering grass . . . all the way back to the tree house.

Annie put Teddy in the leather bag. She and Jack climbed up the rope ladder.

They looked out the window one last time. The ocean of grass was golden in the early sunlight.

By now, the Lakota are walking west, Jack thought.

"Soon everything will change," he said sadly. "The buffalo will vanish. The old way of life for the Lakota will vanish, too."

"But the Great Spirit won't ever vanish," said Annie. "It will *always* take care of Black Hawk's people."

Jack smiled. Annie's words made him feel better.

Arf, arf! Teddy barked, as if to say *Let's go!*

"Okay, okay," said Jack.

He picked up the Pennsylvania book and pointed at a picture of Frog Creek.

"I wish we could go home to our people," he said.

The wind started to blow.

The tree house started to spin.

It spun faster and faster.

Then everything was still.

Absolutely still.

10
Good Medicine

"We're home," said Annie.

Bright sunlight flooded the tree house. Teddy licked Jack's and Annie's faces. They were back in their jeans and T-shirts.

"Hey, silly," Annie said to the dog. "Now we have the second thing to help free you from your spell."

She took the eagle's feather out of Jack's backpack. She put it on Morgan's note, next to the silver pocket watch from the *Titanic*.

"Now we have our gift from the prairie blue," said Jack. "Let your thoughts rise as high as this feather."

"Hey, I just had a thought!" said Annie.

"What?" said Jack.

"I bet Teddy had something to do with White Buffalo Woman," she said.

"Why?" asked Jack.

"One second Teddy disappeared in the grass. Then White Buffalo Woman appeared," said Annie. "When White Buffalo Woman disappeared, Teddy appeared."

"Hmm . . ." said Jack. He stared at the little dog.

Teddy tilted his head and gave Jack a wise look.

"Well . . ." said Jack, "maybe Teddy has good medicine."

"*Now* you understand," said Annie, smiling.

"Ja-ack! An-nie!" A call came from the distance.

Jack and Annie looked out the window of the tree house.

Their mom and their grandmother were standing on their porch.

"Yay, Grandmother's here!" said Annie.

"We're coming!" they shouted together.

"Let's put Teddy in your backpack," said Annie. "So we can take him home with us this time."

"Okay," said Jack.

But when they turned around, the little dog was gone.

"Teddy?" said Annie.

There was no sign of him.

"Oh, man, as soon as we turned our backs,

he slipped away," said Jack. "Just like last time."

"Don't worry," said Annie. "He'll find us again soon. I'm sure of it." She started down the rope ladder.

Jack grabbed his pack and followed.

As they started for home, a wind gusted through the trees.

Jack stopped for a moment to look at the woods.

Branches waved their leaves.

Birds left the branches and swooped up into the blue sky.

Black Hawk's grandmother is right, he thought. *All things are related.*

"Jack!" called Annie.

"Coming!" said Jack.

He hurried to catch up with her.

Together they ran out of the Frog Creek woods . . . up their street . . . and into their own grandmother's arms.

THE LEGEND OF
WHITE BUFFALO WOMAN

Long ago, when the Lakota had no game to hunt, a beautiful woman in white buckskins appeared. She gave the chief of the tribe a special pipe. It had a buffalo carved on its round bowl and eagle feathers hanging from its long wooden stem.

White Buffalo Woman told the chief that the smoke from the sacred pipe would carry prayers to the Great Spirit. The Great Spirit would answer by helping the Lakota find buffalo to hunt.

White Buffalo Woman also said that the pipe smoke would join all living things to the Lakota tribe.

The pipe bowl represented the earth.

The buffalo carved upon it represented all four-legged animals that live upon the earth.

The pipe's wooden stem represented all that grows on the earth.

The twelve eagle feathers hanging from it represented all the winged creatures.

As White Buffalo Woman walked away from the tribe, she turned into a white buffalo calf— one of the rarest animals of all.

The legend of White Buffalo Woman has been handed down from generation to generation by Lakota people.

MORE FACTS FOR YOU AND JACK

1) The Lakota tribe has also been called the Sioux.

2) Today most Lakota live on reservations in North and South Dakota. ("Reservations" are areas of land reserved for Native Americans by the U.S. government.) Lakota parents and grandparents still pass on the traditional beliefs of their people to their children.

3) The true name of the buffalo is *bison*. Bison came to North America during the Ice Age and at one time were the biggest group of large mammals on the continent.

4) In the 1800s, the U.S. Army was at war with the Native Americans of the plains.

They knew the Native American way of life could not survive without the bison. So they decided to kill all the herds. In the years that followed, millions of bison were killed until there were only a few hundred left.

5) In the early 1900s, many people were upset by the killing of the bison. They asked the government to help save these animals. Captive bison were sent to Yellowstone National Park and protected from hunters. Almost 2,500 bison live there today.

Have you read the Magic Tree House book
in which Jack and Annie find themselves sinking
on a doomed ship?

MAGIC TREE HOUSE® #17

TONIGHT ON THE
TITANIC

Don't miss the next Magic Tree House book,
in which Jack and Annie meet ferocious
tigers in the jungle of India . . .

MAGIC TREE HOUSE® #19

TIGERS AT
TWILIGHT

Discover the facts
behind the fiction with the

MAGIC TREE HOUSE®
RESEARCH GUIDES

The must-have, all-true companions for your
favorite Magic Tree House® adventures!

AROUND THE WORLD WITH JACK AND ANNIE

Get your
Official
Magic Tree House
PASSPORT!
www.magictreehouse.com

Around the World with Jack and Annie!

You have traveled to faraway places and have been
on countless Magic Tree House adventures.
Now is your chance to receive an official
Magic Tree House passport and collect official stamps
for each destination from around the world!

HOW

Get your exclusive Magic Tree House Passport!*

Send your name, street address, city, state, zip code, and date of birth to:
The Magic Tree House Passport, Random House Children's Books,
Marketing Department, 1745 Broadway, 10th Floor, New York, NY 10019

OR log on to **www.magictreehouse.com**
to download and print your passport now!

Collect Official Magic Tree House Stamps:

Log on to **www.magictreehouse.com** to submit your answers to the
trivia questions below. If you answer correctly, you will automatically
receive your official stamp for Book 18: *Buffalo Before Breakfast*.

**1. What was the largest North American tribe
in the Great Plains in the 1800s?**

2. What does it mean to hold up two fingers in the Lakota tribe?

3. What is Jack's Lakota name?

Read all the Magic Tree House adventures for a chance to collect them all! RHCB

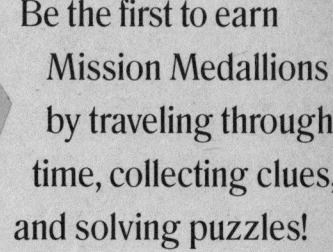

Guess what?
Jack and Annie have a musical CD!

For more information about
MAGIC TREE HOUSE: THE MUSICAL
(including how to order the CD!),
visit www.mthmusical.com.